Karen and Brett at

326 Harper's Cove

The Harper's Cove Series

by
Deanndra Hall

Karen and Brett at 326 Harper's Cove
The Harper's Cove Series

Copyright © 2013 Deanndra Hall
ISBN-13: 978-0615958927
ISBN-10: 0615958923
Print Edition

Celtic Muse Publishing, LLC
P.O. Box 3722
Paducah, KY 42002-3722

All rights reserved. Except as permitted under the U.S. Copyright Act of 1976, no part of this publication may be reproduced, distributed, or transmitted in any form or by any means, or stored in a database or retrieval system, without the prior written permission of the author.

This book is a work of fiction.

Names of characters, places, and events are the construction of the author, except those locations that are well-known and of general knowledge, and all are used fictitiously. Any resemblance to persons living or dead is coincidental, and great care was taken to design places, locations, or businesses that fit into the regional landscape without actual identification; as such, resemblance to actual places, locations, or businesses is coincidental. Any mention of a branded item, artistic work, or well-known business establishment, is used for authenticity in the work of fiction and was chosen by the author because of personal preference, its high quality, or the authenticity it lends to the work of fiction; the author has received no remuneration, either monetary or in-kind, for use of said product names, artistic work, or business establishments, and mention is not intended as advertising, nor does it constitute an endorsement. The author is solely responsible for content.

Cover design 2013 M.D. Halliman, used by permission of the artist.
Formatting by BB eBooks

Disclaimer:

Material in this work of fiction is of a graphic sexual nature and is not intended for audiences under 18 years of age.

More titles from this author:

Love Under Construction Series

The Groundbreaking (Free Introductory Volume) – Summer 2013

The Groundbreaking is a preview of the main characters contained in all of the Love Under Construction Series books. Not intended as a work of erotic fiction, it is simply a way for the reader to get to know and love each character by discovering their backgrounds. Contains graphic situations that are unsuitable for readers under 18 years old.

Laying a Foundation (Book 1) – Fall 2013

Sometimes death robs us of the life we thought we'd have; sometimes a relationship that just won't die can be almost as bad. And sometimes the universe aligns to take care of everything. When you've spent years alone, regardless the circumstances, getting back out there can be hard. But when you've finally opened up to love and it looks like you might lose it all, can love be enough to see you through?

Tearing Down Walls (Book 2) – Fall 2013

Secrets – they can do more damage than the truth. Secrets have kept two people from realizing their full potential, but even worse, have kept them from forming lasting relationships and finding the love and acceptance they both desperately need. Can they finally let go of those secrets in time to find love – and maybe even to stay alive?

Renovating a Heart (Book 3) – Spring 2014

Can a person's past really be so bad that they can never recover from it? Sometimes it seems that way. One man hides the truth of a horrific loss in his teen years; one woman hides the truth of a broken, scarred life that took a wrong turn in her teens. Can they be honest with each other, or even with themselves, about their feelings? And will they be able to go that distance before one of them is lost forever?

Planning an Addition (Book 4) – Fall 2014

When you think you're set for life and that life gets yanked out from under you, starting over is hard. One woman who's starting over finds herself in love with two men who've started over too, and she's forced to choose. Or is she? And when one of them is threatened by their past, everyone has choices to make. Can they make the right ones in time to save a life?

The Harper's Cove Series

Beginning with the flagship volume, *Karen and Brett at 326 Harper's Cove*, find out exactly what the neighbors of Harper's Cove are up to when they go inside and close their doors. According to Gloria, the drunken busy-body of the cove, they're all up to something perverse, and she's determined to find out their secrets. As she sneaks, peeks, pokes, and prods, her long-suffering husband, Russell, begs her to leave all of their nice neighbors alone. But could Gloria be right?

The Harper's Cove series books are fast, fun, nasty little reads priced just right to provide a quick, naughty romp. See if the neighbors of Harper's Cove shock you just enough to find out what the occupants of the next address will do!

Karen and Brett at 326 Harper's Cove

Gloria wants more than anything to be invited to one of Karen and Brett Reynolds' parties, and she's very vocal about it. Karen and Brett, however, know full well that if Gloria were ever invited to one of their parties, she would be in a hurry to leave, and in an even bigger hurry to let everyone know they are the scourge of the neighborhood. Every Saturday night, Karen and Brett keep their secrets – all twelve of them.

Donna and Connor at 228 Harper's Cove

Those nice people at 228, the Millicans? They're religious counselors, trying to help lovely couples who are having marital problems. Problem is, they're not counseling; training, maybe, but not counseling. But no matter what Donna says, Gloria still thinks the truck that delivered large crates to the Millicans' house in the wee hours of the morning, two weeks after they'd moved in, was pretty suspicious. Donna says it was exercise equipment that the moving company had lost, but Gloria's not so sure. Could it be that they're not as they appear?

Becca and Greg at 314 Harper's Cove

Even though they're quiet and stay to themselves, Becca and Greg Henderson seem pretty nice and average. They don't go out much or have many people over, except for that one couple who are probably relatives. But when that half-sister of Becca's moves in, it all seems a little fishy; she gets around pretty well for a person recovering from cancer. And where was Becca going all decked out in that weird outfit? The Henderson are tight-lipped, but Gloria hopes she can eventually get to the bottom of things. If she does, she'll get the biggest surprise of her life.

And we're just getting started!

A word from the author...

Writing novels is my first love. I like nothing better than to take a name, find a photo that represents the face I have for him or her in my mind, assign a birthdate, an occupation, a love interest, family, friends, and sometimes enemies, and let my imagination go wild. If novels didn't take so long to write, I'd crank out one a week!

That's how I got the idea for this series. They're short, quick reads that will get your motor humming and entertain you enough to wonder what the next couple in the cove will be up to. I was trying to figure out a way to plug in some short but quality reading between the volumes of the Love Under Construction series, and along came Karen and Brett and blew me away! I couldn't wait to get started on this series, and I think it'll be different from anything you've read before.

Thanks to my long-suffering partner, who thought I'd take a break after the first novel was written (what's wrong with him?), and to the people who've taken the time to dive into the Walters' world. I'll be sorry when I write the last word of that series; I'll miss them like they were family. A big thank you to my betas. And a big, big thank you to the technical people: my handy-dandy photographer; my fellow writers (especially some folks who live over in Clayfield); and my conversion company, BB eBooks. The staff at BB has probably saved my life, and at the very least my sanity, not to mention my hair.

Take a stroll down Harper's Cove and see what's going on. Better luck than Gloria's had. And try not to be too judgmental; we've all got skeletons in our closets.

Love and happy reading,
Deanndra

Visit me at: www.deanndrahall.com

Connect with me on my:
http://substance-b.com/DeanndraHall.html

Contact me at: DeanndraHall@gmail.com

Join me on Facebook at: facebook.com/deanndra.hall

Catch me on Twitter at: twitter.com/DeanndraHall

Find me blogging at: deanndrahall.blogspot.com

Write to me at: P.O. Box 3722, Paducah, KY 42002-3722

Support your Indie authors!

Independent (Indie) authors are not a new phenomenon, but they are a hard-working one. As Indie authors, we write our books, have trouble finding anyone to beta read them for us, seldom have money to hire an editor, struggle with our cover art, find it nearly impossible to get a reviewer to even glance at our books, and do all of our own publicity, promotion, and marketing. This is not something that we do until we find someone to offer us a contract – this is a conscious decision we've made to do for ourselves that which we'd have to do regardless (especially promotion, which publishers rarely do anyway). We do it so big publishing doesn't take our money and give us nothing in return. We do it because we do not want to give up rights to something on which we've worked so hard. And we do it because we want to offer you a convenient, quality product for an excellent price.

Indie authors try to bring their readers something fresh, fun, and different. Please help your Indie authors:

- Buy our books! That makes it possible for us to continue to produce them;

- If you like them, please go back to the retailer from which you bought them and review them for us. That helps us more than you could know;
- If you like them, please tell your friends, relatives, nail tech, lawn care guy, anyone you can find, about our books. Recommend them, please;
- If you're in a book circle, always contact an Indie author to see if you can get free or discounted books to use in your circle. Many would love to help you out;
- If you see our books being pirated, please let us know. We worked weekends, holidays, and through vacations (if we even get one) to put these books out, so please report it if you see them being stolen.

More than anything else, we hope you enjoy our books and, if you do, please contact us in whatever manner we've provided as it suits you. Visit our blogs and websites, friend our Facebook sites, and follow us on Twitter. We'd love to get to know you!

Karen and Brett at

326 Harper's Cove

CHAPTER ONE

Gloria

I keep trying to catch Karen outside. I know they're up to something; I just don't know what.

Russell keeps saying, "Gloria, leave those people alone. They're not bothering us, and you shouldn't bother them." And he usually follows it up with, "And lay off the booze."

I don't drink that much, really. I usually don't have anything until about one o'clock. Well, sometimes at ten thirty. One day, at nine. But that was just once. And I'd had a bad week.

But I know something's going on over there. They have these parties every week. I've asked, but she's really tight-lipped about them. We never get invited, and I don't know why. I've always been friendly to them, but they never invite us. Nobody does. Greg and Becca down the street? They never have people over. Never. If they did, I bet they'd invite us.

I've even tried sneaking over there to see if I could find out what's going on, but they keep the shades drawn. When those people come over, Karen and Brett turn on all of those outside lights they have, and I can't sneak over there – someone could see me. I think they're afraid of burglars or something. And that means I can't get close enough to hear anything. One of these days, though, I'll find out. They'll slip up, leave the door open or something, and I'll be able to see inside. Then I'll know. I bet they're gambling or smoking marijuana or something.

One time, I walked over that way after the garbage truck had come because I saw something in the street. It was a rubber. I told Russell, I said, "Russell, there was a rubber in the street in front of the Reynolds' house."

And you know what he said? He said, "Gloria, you don't know where that came from. It could've come from that garbage truck for all you know." But I know it came from their garbage. Filthy thing.

I told Russell, "They're having sex with rubbers. Why would they do that?"

He just looked at me and said, "It's none of our business. Maybe she's allergic to the pill. Besides, they don't call them that anymore; they call them condoms." Smart-aleck. And then he said, "And lay off the sauce."

Damn it. Doesn't anybody else care if the neighborhood is going to hell in a hand basket?

CHAPTER TWO

Karen

I've told Brett at least ten times that we've got to get new sheets. Eight sets just aren't enough – we need at least ten, maybe twelve.

Since it's Friday night, we've only got tomorrow to get the house in order before everybody starts showing up. There are a million things to do, and I can't seem to get to any of them as fast as I'd like. The floors need to be cleaned up, bathrooms stocked, baskets of supplies set out, air mattresses blown up. And he wants to watch the game. Un-frickin'-believable.

To make matters worse, I can't even go to the garbage can without that damn Gloria from down the street stopping me to yak. She's got to be the nosiest bitch I've ever met.

"Karen! Hey, Karen! How're you?" She comes running up the driveway; I use the term "running" loosely because she's so damn dumpy that she can't move very fast. And that crazy hair – doesn't she own a brush?

"I'm good, Gloria. Really busy." I try to ignore her, but she just won't be ignored. Worse yet, I can smell the booze on her and, with it just being Friday, god knows what she'll be like by tomorrow. "Can't talk right now." I try to make it back to the porch, but she beats me to it and gets between me and the steps.

"So I guess you know about the Warrens, huh? Such a shame," she drones.

"No, I don't know about the Warrens." I really do, but I'm not about to tell her and I really don't want to get into a conversation about them, so I take the self-righteous twist and turn it on her. "I don't gossip – never have, never will. Now if you'll excuse me . . ."

"Wait! But they're so . . ."

I try again. "Not kidding, Gloria. If you want to gossip, you'd better go to another front porch, because mine is closed for that stuff. My mother always said, 'If they'll talk to you about someone, they'll talk to someone about you.' So my policy is don't see it, don't say it, and don't hear it, and you can't tell it." I walk past her and up the steps.

"Got anything exciting going on this weekend?" she asks like she always does, changing gears when I won't play into her game.

"Yes. Having a party," I lie.

"Gee, you guys sure throw a lot of those. What's it take to get an invitation to one of those things?"

"You have to be friends with us. Now if you'll excuse me..." I dart through the front door. Behind me she's saying something about being friends, but I don't respond, just close the door.

"Don't tell me – Miss Gossip Bottle," Brett asks when I get back inside.

"Yeah. Hinted around that she wanted an invitation to our 'party.' She wouldn't if she knew more about it."

Brett laughs. "You've got that right!" He's still chuckling when I head for the bathroom, bowl brush in hand.

"Hi!" Belinda and Joe are the first ones in the door on Saturday evening. "I'll put this in there and be right back." She carries the container into the kitchen; probably her peanut butter cookies. Those things are favorites within our group. When she comes back, she kisses me. I love that about Belinda; she doesn't go straight for tongue, just a nice, warm kiss. And she's so lovely, those big brown eyes and that wavy, dark hair. And nice boobs too. Then she kisses Brett. I love watching him kiss her, but I don't get much of a chance because Joe kisses me, then buries his face in my neck and nips me gently.

"Guys, guys! Wait for everyone else, please!" I admonish, but I'm laughing as I do it. Before the words are completely out of my mouth, Angela and Juan come laughing through the door. As soon as he sees me, Juan grabs me around the waist and plants a big one right on my lips, then forces his tongue into my mouth, and I feel rocket engines ignite in my undies. He's so positively yummy that I think about him all week until the next; hell, I think about them all. Angela kisses Brett and then Joe, and Juan breaks away from me and gives Belinda a quick peck on the lips. I can't help but want him to kiss me again.

Before long, Daniel and Katie have come in, followed closely by Heather and Josh, who are the newest couple to join us. Josh is the youngest guy in the group, and definitely lacking in the experience realm but, christ, he's so damn good-looking that I can overlook most everything else, especially when I get to look up at him. We'll take care of that experience thing eventually.

Carson and Gilea are the last ones here. Carson is just fucking beautiful, no other way to put it. Tall, blond, icy blue eyes, and so sinewy and statuesque. They make such an odd couple, with Gilea easily the heaviest woman in our group and so round and cheerful-looking. And did I mention her tits? They're *huge*. All the guys love them.

After everyone has greeted everyone, I ask them all to come in and sit down. That's when Katie looks around and says, "Where are David and Holly?"

"Yeah, I wanted to talk to you about them before we start," Brett says to the group. "I don't know how many of you know this, but David lost his job. And it's been awhile but they didn't say anything to anyone." There's a collective gasp. "It looks like they might lose their house, and I really don't want to lose them."

"So what can we do?" Joe asks. That's so like Joe; always willing to jump in and help.

"Does anyone know of any job openings?"

Daniel immediately blurts out, "Sure!" Everyone kind of jumps. He never says much, but when he does, it's usually something important. "I'm in charge of hiring for the new project. I'd be glad to hire him on."

My eyes start to tear up, and Brett almost chokes; the rest of the room is sniffling. "Please call him as soon as you get a chance and tell him. I know he and Holly would appreciate that. They're good people, and he's a hard worker." Daniel nods, and Brett looks at me with a smile. That's what I love about all of us; it's all for one and one for all with this bunch.

"Okay," I say. "Enough of the somber stuff. Let the fun begin!"

I've never seen people come out of their clothes so fast. But I'm one to talk; I'm already peeling off my jeans and pulling my tee over my head. First one undressed is Josh; just like a twenty-something. And this time he makes a bee-line to me. "Karen, teach me something new," he whispers in my ear as his hands wind around me and grip my ass, his fingers digging into my cheeks.

I hear a moan and turn; Belinda's already going down on Brett and it's obvious he loves it. Hearing my gorgeous guy, happily sexed up, that chestnut hair tucked behind his ear and his easy-to-follow happy trail front and center, turns me on, and I reach down and start stroking Josh. He may be the youngest guy here, but he's not the smallest by any measure, big enough around to cause a burn and long enough to smack a cervix hard. I start to wonder what I might be able to teach him when Joe comes up behind me, reaches around, and cups my breasts in his hands. When he does, Josh bends down and takes a nipple in his mouth, and I start to lose track of who's doing what. When I finally look around again, Brett's face-down in Gilea's slit, her eyes closed and her hips twitching, spread-eagle on our dining room table.

"Josh wants me to teach him something new, Joe. Got any suggestions?"

"What have you never done, kid?" Joe asks him as he twists the nipple Josh isn't sucking between his thumb and index finger, and I feel my pussy throb. That guy – Joe is one of the sexiest men I've ever met. Deep, dark voice, that almost-black hair with the gray at the temples, tanned beyond belief, and let me tell you, he knows how to please a woman. Belinda is one lucky lady.

"I'd kinda like to learn how to fuck an ass – correctly, that is," Josh answers from around my nipple. I don't know if it's the words or the actions, but I'm tingling all over. "I don't want to hurt her."

Joe motions for pretty little Heather to come to him. She's been across the room kissing Gilea, and Gilea's been fingering her while Brett sucks and pulls on Gilea's clit like he just can't get enough. Heather stops the kissing and comes over to us, her spiky, blond hair wild and crazy. When she does, I see Angela scoot under the table and take Brett's cock into her mouth, letting him rock into her while he keeps it up on Gilea.

"Hey, handsome, what's up?" Heather purrs and strokes Joe's cock with her small, soft hand. It's a beautiful thing to watch, Joe's giant cock getting hard and then harder, and then harder still.

"Your guy here wants to learn to fuck you in the ass. So Karen and I will teach you both. Karen will let Josh fuck her ass while I fuck yours and he watches. You'll learn to take it, and he'll learn to give it. Sound good?"

Heather has an odd look on her face. "I'm not sure I want to . . ."

Josh looks at her and scowls. "I'm gonna fuck your ass one way or another, baby. If I were you, I'd prefer to learn how with someone who knows what they're doing as opposed to having me go in cold." Heather shivers a little, and I see Joe frown.

"We won't do it unless you want it, but I've gotta tell ya, I'd love to be buried in that beautiful thing." Joe smiles at her and kisses her. When he does, I see him shove two fingers into her pussy and she almost melts. "Wow – you're slick as ice, baby. I think you want me to, don't you?" Heather nods to him. It hasn't escaped me that Joe can get a woman to do pretty much anything he wants – sure as hell works on me anyway. "Okay, let's get to it. I'm too damn hard to wait." The four of us go to the nearest air mattress. "Both of you girls get on your knees on the edge of the mattress. Baby," he says and smacks my ass playfully, "I'm just giving direction for their benefit; I know from experience that you know what you're doing." He winks when he says it, then looks at Josh. "Get one of those and suit up," he says as he points to the basket beside the mattress. Josh takes out a condom, then tosses one to Joe, and they both roll them on, then Joe adds, "And I'd advise you to always use a condom when you go into an ass. Keeps you from having to spend precious fucking time cleaning yourself up." Then Josh reaches for the bottle of lube and hands it to Joe.

I hear the "snap" of the flip-top lid and watch as lube makes a shiny river down Heather's ass crack and onto the floor, and she shivers and bows her back. Within seconds I feel it running down mine too; I know what's coming and I can barely wait. I watch as Joe presses a finger into Heather's rosette and she whines, and I feel Josh do the same to me. He pumps his finger in and out of me while he watches Joe with Heather, and I hear the younger woman moan, then cry out when Joe takes out his finger and replaces it with two in her nasty little back door. I feel the exquisite stretch when Josh does the same to me. And he's so damn young, he'll last forever. This'll be good.

As Josh pumps his fingers in and out of my ass, I look across to see Juan fucking, or maybe speed fucking, Katie, fisting her auburn hair in one hand with his free arm wrapped under her ass. He's pounding her for all he's worth, and she's loving it, I can tell. I see him stiffen and I know he's coming. When he finally does, she's crying out and begging him to keep going. He says something to her, and when he steps away, Carson takes over, pounding her like a pile driver. Angela reaches immediately for Juan and takes his cock in her hand, and he's on her like ketchup on fries in a split second. I'd like to keep watching, but I feel Josh's fingers pull out and I know Joe's about to talk him into me.

"Watch. Press the head in like this." Joe presses the head of his cock – did I say substantial cock? because it's impressively substantial – against Heather's asshole, and I see her squirm. He grabs her hips to hold her still and presses until the head pops into her. She lets out a cry and shakes her head. I feel the head of Josh's cock breach my tightness, and I can't help but moan. God, I love a good ass fucking. "Let me in, baby," I hear Joe say and Heather shakes her head again. "You'll let me in," he says a little more forcefully, and he draws his hand back and slaps her hard on the ass. She lets out a surprised little cry, and he pushes another thick, rigid inch into her tight little asshole.

"So take it slow on the way in the first couple of times. After that, pick up speed. Kind of feel her out. She'll let you know if it's just too much," Joe tells Josh. "You need to honor that – the first couple of times. After that, do the same thing, but get vigorous. If she complains that it hurts but she still lets you do it, it means she really wants it. And in this case, practice makes perfect." I feel Josh pushing forward into me, and I push back into him, giving him more, letting him know I want it, and he moans loudly and keeps slipping into me. But Heather is having a hard time of it. She's crying out with every quarter inch Joe manages to get into her. When Josh is completely buried in my ass up to his balls, I look over at Heather. Her face is screwed up and she looks like she's going to cry. So I say the only thing there is to say, really: "Joe, fuck into her. Go ahead and get it all in. If she's going to take it, it's time – just do it." It's like ripping off a bandage. If you've got a partner who knows what he's doing and won't hurt you, it's best to just get it over with.

I see Heather's face cloud but she nods, and then Joe pulls back ever-so-slightly before shoving straight into her tight hole. She lets out a shriek and everyone in the room – and I do mean everyone – stops what they're doing and turns to look at her. But before the echo of the shriek has died, Joe draws back and shoves in again. This time Heather moans loudly, and I see most of the faces in the room smile. The only ones who aren't smiling are wishing it were them pushing into her virgin ass, and that makes *me* smile. Josh draws back and then slams into me, and I moan loudly and shake. For someone who's barely past being a kid, he's got quite an impressive dick.

Before long, both of the men are pounding into us, and Heather has tears running down her face. I know she's hurting, but I also know that tomorrow she'll be glad she did this, especially when Josh has had me, because he's going to want more. He's going to want to fuck her ass tomorrow and at least she'll know to hold still for him and let him in.

Joe has amazing self-control and, even though it's obvious Josh is about to shoot into his condom, Joe is nowhere near finished with Heather. He's still stroking into her and she's still hanging in there, her cheeks wet with tears. Bless his heart, he's asked her twice if she wants to stop and she's said no both times, so he keeps going. When Josh finally finishes off in me, I tell him, "Go over to Heather and start stroking her clit. If you can make her come while Joe's fucking her, it'll be better for her." He takes my advice and, before I can find someone else to screw, she's headed at breakneck speed toward her orgasm. I find myself wishing I could watch her explode.

But before I can think, Juan motions for me. When I get to him, his manhood is pointing straight up like a flagpole. He points to a mattress, lies down, and growls, "Mount me." I do it without even thinking about it; it's a treat. Juan's cock isn't especially long, but it's thick, and I love the stretch. Before I can get comfortably seated on it, Gilea comes to me and starts sucking one nipple and twisting the other one; I swear, I think that girl likes the women better than the men, which is, of course, okay with me. I can't hold it back, and I let out a long, low moan. That gets Carson's attention, and he comes toward us. I see Juan smile at him and I'm pretty sure I know what's coming. Juan takes my hands and draws them up and behind his head. "Hold them there, honey; don't make me tie you up," he whispers as he laughs, his full, soft lips against my ear, and everything in me shivers. He knows I realize what they're doing and there's no chance I'll mess it up. I want it, want it bad. Once he has my wrists gripped tight, he looks at Carson and says, "Get in there."

Carson pushes hard and sinks himself into me and, even though I just got finished with one ass fucking, the burn comes back. With Juan's thick cock already in my pussy, the double penetration is exquisite, a pain I'll crave for weeks. Brett comes over to watch us, and he looks impressed. I can tell he's going to want this later, and I smile up at him. He's smiling back. "Baby, that's a beautiful thing to watch," he whispers to me, then leans down between all of the bodies surrounding me and kisses me. I'm glad he's getting off watching us. It's a bonus.

Juan backs out, and Carson burrows into my ass up to his balls. He's the only one of the guys who doesn't shave smooth, and his fur tickles my ass. Then he pulls out and Juan strokes back in. It's good – really, really good. I don't want to, but I cry out – I can't help it. And just when I think I can't take any more, Juan reaches back, takes my arms from around his neck, and pushes me upright. Carson has to work to stroke – it's not as easy as it was when I was lying forward on Juan – but he's managing, and Juan goes straight for my clit. When he does, I can't help but shriek, and he works it like he owns it.

I'm right on the edge, hovering, loving every minute of it, wanting it and not wanting it because I don't want it to end, and then it's there, spangles behind my eyelids, my breath catching in my throat, and I'm screaming, can't help it. I hear Brett whispering, "Do it, baby! Do it. God, this is good. Take it, baby!" Juan keeps stroking, and I keep shaking. I can't stop. He finally stops and I would collapse on him, but while I was coming, Carson had wrapped his arms around me and cupped a breast in each hand, and he's working my nipples over like they're his prized possessions. Juan barks at him, "Let her go!" and I drop onto Juan's chest, exhausted.

"Now – fuck her hard." Carson doesn't need to be told twice. Juan's big cock is buried in me and

Carson's hitting just the right spot, and I'm falling into it, the burn taking me over, and before I realize what's happening, I'm coming again, jerking against Juan's chest, and he's gripping me to him so I can't move, which makes it even more powerful. God, I've never done anything that was this intense, so delightfully painful, so forbidden and craved. I'm just screaming now, and pretty much everybody has come to watch and cheer us on. I can hear them laughing and whispering, talking about how hard Carson's pounding me and how Juan's restraining me, but I don't care. This is more than I could've ever asked for, hoped for. It's past heavenly. It's way past mind-blowing. I don't even know how to describe it, just the best damn pain I've ever known in my life.

I feel Carson stiffen and I know he's done. Sure enough, within seconds he drops onto my back, panting. I hear Juan say, "Hey, bud, get out and over. I need to get off too." When Carson pulls out of me and drops onto the mattress beside Juan and me, Juan flips me over and away from Carson, then begins to pound into my pussy, looking for his own release. I feel another orgasm building, and I reach down and start to stroke my clit while he strokes into me.

When I come, I'm in control, and I just keep going, pulsing tightly around Juan's cock. He whispers into my neck, "Damn, Karen, you're a fine fuck." I'm still stroking myself and my hips are still rocking upward when I feel his cock thicken and lengthen, and he comes royally inside me, then drops onto me and grinds into me, his hands wrapped around to grip my ass. I can't stroke myself anymore with him on top of me, so I work to get my arm out from between us.

I'm exhausted, and all I can manage to say is "Jesus christ, you guys are good fucks, you know that?" I ruffle Juan's short, dark hair and he laughs, then I reach over and stroke Carson's cock and he moans. I'm finally lucid enough to look around, and I see that Brett's balls-deep in Belinda's ass and, in front of her, Joe's fucking into her mouth. Juan rolls off of me and, before he can move, Angela goes down on him, smiling around his dick as it stiffens again immediately. She's told us that they fuck each other at least three times a day, and it shows – she knows just how to push his buttons.

Carson's reaching for another condom and as soon as he gets the new one on, Katie mounts him and starts riding him like a bronco at the rodeo. Her tits are so beautiful, so pert and round and plump against that hard, lean body.

I'm wondering who's free when Daniel asks me, "Karen, can I fuck your face? I was watching you guys – that was awesome." His cock is in his hand

and it's raging and purple, a beautiful thing with its own pulse and, at that size, probably its own zip code.

"Of course, sweetie. I'll swallow for you." Actually, my mouth waters just thinking about it. I've only gone down on Daniel once before, and his cum is the tastiest I've ever had. It's kind of sweet – Katie says they eat a lot of fruit, and he told me the last time that he made sure to eat some pineapple before he came over. That's gotta be it. When I take him in my mouth, some of it is still on his dick, and I lick it like an ice cream cone. I can't remember who I saw him in before me.

That's when I look up and see it – he's got a look on his face like he's the biggest, baddest Dom on the planet and I'm his slutty little sub. He's a beautiful guy, finely chiseled features, wavy dark hair pulled back into a short ponytail, and dark, sultry eyes. I'm not sucking him as a favor to him – he's actually gracing me with the honor of sucking him, and I know it. I feel like the luckiest woman on the planet when he looks at me like that. I go at it with gusto and wonder how long he'll leave me on my own with his manhood.

And then it happens – he grabs my hair on either side of my head and drives himself into my throat. For a split second, I think I'm going to choke, and then he sets up the rhythm. It's beyond delicious. I can feel my throat expanding every time his cock pushes down into it, and I wonder if he can see it until he says, "I love seeing your throat swell with my cock head. Come over here." He pulls out of my mouth, leads me to the dining room table, and has me lie across it on my back. "Scoot toward me," he orders, and pulls me far enough toward him that my head is hanging off the edge. I know exactly what's about to happen, and the thought makes my pussy gush and my head spin. He reaches for my hands and grips my wrists tightly against his palms.

I open my mouth, and he slams in – all the way in. With my head back, he's got a straight shot into my throat, and I know I'm not in control anymore. I want to push him away, but he's holding my wrists so I'm completely at his mercy, which only makes every sensation that much more electrifying. He sets up a rhythm again, and I feel myself slipping away, at least until I feel somebody lick up my slit, and then they're sucking and tugging on my clit, circling it with their tongue, and I'm so confused and blissed out that I slip into that place I've only been a couple of times. One of our old lovers who moved away, James, was really into BDSM, and he called it subspace. I don't know exactly what it is, but it's a damn good place to be.

I hear Daniel say, "Oh my god, look at that. My cock is filling up her throat." I hear somebody else say, "Shit, that's hot! Look at that!" I think I hear birds chirping and angels singing until Daniel snarls, "Swallow, cunt. Swallow around me." I love hearing him talk so dirty to me and call me names, and I feel his seed shoot down my throat and come back up into my mouth, its salty bitterness, its heat, and he stops with his cock lodged in my throat. I can't breathe and I start to feel dizzy, but I'm not panicked – I trust him. Just as I'm about to black out, I feel my airway open up and I heave in a breath and swallow anything left in my mouth and throat. God, he's delectable.

That's when I get a chance to look down, and I see it's Brett face down in my bits, holding my hips and thighs against the table. He's working it for all he's worth, and I feel the coiling in my gut. Before I can moan, Daniel leans down and kisses me deeply. "I love tasting myself on a woman's lips," he whispers, and that's it for me – I come viciously. Brett won't let up, and Daniel won't turn me loose, his tongue still buried in my mouth. I can't cry out, can't moan, all I can do is feel the spasms, the churning behind my clit, my pussy clenching and releasing over and over.

Before he stops, Brett starts speed finger fucking me, pressing into my G-spot. Daniel moves his mouth away, and I hear Brett laugh and say, "Hey, guys, get out of the way – she's gonna blow!" I relax and let it come to me, balled up and beautiful, and in seconds I turn loose with a stream of ejac that shoots out, how far I don't know. I hear a couple of the guys cheer.

"Damn, wish you'd do that," I hear Carson say to Gilea.

"I would if you knew what you were doing," she bites back.

"Ouch!" he laughs.

I'm gasping, and I hear Joe say, "Let Brett teach you, bud. That's why we're here, remember?"

Brett climbs up onto the table and whispers to me, "That was great, baby. I love you."

"I love you too," I whisper back to him and kiss him. I can taste one of the other ladies on his mouth, and it makes me so hot I want to fuck him right then and there. But I hear him tell Carson they can take Gilea over to another spot and he'll teach Carson to make her squirt, as the guys are so fond of calling it.

I find myself lying on the table alone. When I'm finally able to sit up and take stock of myself, I realize everybody is winding down. Belinda looks like she's been fucked one too many times, and I don't think Juan could get it up again if his life depended on it. Daniel's sitting on the mattress nearest me, and I get off the table, go over to him, and lie down, then pull him down to lie beside me.

Just as his arms encircle me, there's somebody on his other side – Heather. He rolls onto his back and puts his other arm around her, drawing us both up until our heads are resting on his chest. He kisses her forehead and then mine. "You girls know I love you, don't you?"

"Um-hum. I love you too," I tell him and kiss him. "And I love you too, Heather." She reaches across Daniel and strokes the side of my face, and I grab her hand and kiss her palm. That's when I just can't hold it in anymore; I start to cry.

"What's wrong, sweetie?" Daniel asks me.

"I miss David and Holly tonight." He kisses my forehead again. "Thanks for giving David a job. I hope he'll take it and it's a good fit for him. I don't want to lose them. I love them both."

"We all do," Heather whispers. "I don't want to lose anybody here. I love every person in this room, and I know they love me."

"We all do," Daniel says and kisses her on the forehead.

"Honey, I hope you didn't think Joe and I were being too hard on you while ago," I say to her, reaching to stroke the side of her face.

She shakes her head against Daniel's chest. "No, it's okay, really. I mean, it hurt, but I know I need to learn to do it, especially since all of the guys expect it, so it's okay. It'll just take some getting used to, that's all. But now I'm not afraid to let Josh do it at home. I watched him fuck you so I know he knows how. And you liked it so much – I want to like it that much too."

"You will, baby, with practice."

"Yes, you will," Daniel echoes. "Next time let me ass fuck you. Katie says I'm really good. She had a hard time taking it at first too, but she loves it now. You'll see – it won't take long."

I hear giggling and look over to see Belinda sandwiched between Brett and Carson. Joe's sitting on the mattress that's scooted up to the sofa, and he's leaning back on the front of the sofa, holding Katie close and kissing her like they were fifteen. When I finally spot Angela, Josh has her up in a suspended congress, pressed against the wall and stroking into her slowly while she moans and kisses him. Gilea and Juan are cuddling on another mattress, talking low and giggling softly.

I try to remember how the couples came to the group. Each meeting has some kind of story, some personal, intimate history between all of us. It's lovely and sweet, and we all fit together like pieces of a puzzle. As everyone mellows out, the guys start helping the ladies clean themselves up. Towels go all around, and everyone is looking for their clothes. Belinda and Gilea start laughing when they realize they have each other's bras – Belinda is a D-cup and

Gilea is a double F, and it's pretty funny looking when they put them on and realize what they've done. When everyone is almost dressed, Daniel says, "I've got something I need to talk to all of you about."

Everyone turns to look at him. "You know we'd like to get pregnant." Everyone nods. "But out of respect for all of you, Katie's stayed on her birth control pills. So I've, we've, got a favor to ask."

"Go for it," Joe says. "You know we'll help however we can."

Daniel stops for a second, then says, "If you're all agreeable to it, she'd like to stop taking the pill and see what happens. We're hoping with the extra semen she gets over here, it won't take long."

We all look at each other. Brett is the first to speak, and I'm so proud. "I'll gladly do it. I'd be honored. What about the rest of you?"

Joe looks at Belinda, and she nods. "Sure. Not a problem."

"I'd be glad to," Carson adds, and Gilea pats his knee.

"Everyone should have a baby if they want one." Angela starts to cry, and I think about what a hard time they've had. "Would you guys mind trying the same for us?"

"Hell, no! Consider it done!" Josh chimes in, and Katie nods.

Joe gets a wistful look on his face. "Wouldn't it be great if we had a couple of babies? I think that would be fun. I wouldn't mind being a dad."

"But we might never know who..." Daniel started.

"We'd all be his or her dad. No baby would ever be more loved," Brett says and reaches over to take Angela's hand. She starts to cry in earnest, and Carson leans over and puts his arm around her shoulders.

"Well, it's settled. Maybe we'll have a couple of babies before long." Daniel and Juan both are ecstatic. Everyone takes a deep breath and someone starts laughing. Before long, we're all laughing, just like we always do. No one is leaving without feeling thoroughly fucked and extremely happy, and I know we'll all sleep soundly tonight, especially two couples who have some hope they didn't have when they came through the door.

As the last couple drives away, Brett turns to me and takes me in his arms. "Baby, tonight? That was the damn hottest thing I've ever seen. Will you DP with me next week?"

"Hell yeah, sexy. You can shove that thing up me any time you want!" I laugh. He kisses me, and I can't help but fall into him, melt into him, think of all the ways I love him. I don't know any other couple who is as happy as us – well, maybe the ones who just left.

"Did you guys have fun last night?" Gloria is calling as she makes her way toward me. I can't make it ten feet out the door without being spotted and trapped. She's wearing a hideous muumuu-type thing and a pair of flip-flops, and you could see her coming twenty miles away. I cringe. Does she sit in the window and watch for us to come out of our houses? It sure looks that way.

"Yes, we did. We always do." I'm curt but that doesn't deter her at all. She forges ahead.

"So do you guys play games or something?" she asks me, a blank look on her face.

"No, Gloria, we all strip off and fuck each other," I say as sarcastically as I can manage.

Her eyebrows shoot up. "Well, you don't have to be smart with me! I'm just hoping you had a good time, that's all. Ex-cuuuuUUSE ME!" She turns on her heels and stomps off toward her house. Finally – I found a way to shut her up.

When I get back inside, I tell Brett what I did and he laughs for ten minutes. "I can't believe you said that to her!" he gasps.

"Well, it worked!" I make up my mind right then that I'll come up with some other fantastic stories for the next time she starts poking around. But it's really hard to come up with something more fantastic than what we're already doing.

CHAPTER THREE

Gloria

The nerve of her. That was so rude. All I wanted to know was if they had a good time last night, that's all. And then she said the "F" word. Classless. If I hadn't had some cough syrup before I ran into her, I might've been as smart-mouthed as she was. But I'm better than that.

When I tell Russell what she said, he tells me, "Serves you right. Leave those people alone. They're not doing anything to you."

"What if they're doing drugs over there? Still think they're not doing anything to us?"

I can't believe it. He says, "So what if they're doing drugs over there? They're not shitting on our lawn or putting bombs in our mailbox, so it's none of our business what they're doing. Gloria, I swear, leave those people alone or, so help me god, I'm going to send you back to rehab, you hear me?"

Well, looks like I'm the only person in this neighborhood who cares what's going on around me or cares about the safety of the neighborhood. I guess I'm the only one, and it's all up to me. I'll just have to stay on it. I'll find out eventually what they're up to – all of them. One house at a time.

CHAPTER FOUR

Karen

I thought I'd gotten rid of her, but that bitch just won't leave me alone. It's my Saturday to work, and when I get home and go to the mailbox, damn if she doesn't catch me. Same old quizzes. "Having another party tonight?"

"Yes, Gloria, although I wouldn't call them parties. We just sit around and talk. We're just a bunch of friends who like to spend time together. Sometimes we watch a movie, sometimes play a game. It's just a get-together. We all know each other really well, and anyone else would just feel out of place." There – that sounded pretty good.

"I'd love a chance to get to know them all. I bet they're nice people," she says. God, she's determined, I'll say that for her.

"Yeah, well, I've got to go and get the house ready, get the popcorn popped and the dip out. See you around." She'd choke if she knew I was putting out lube, condoms, and antibacterial wipes. I hot-foot it back to the house. I halfway expect her to follow me but, thank god, she doesn't.

When I get back inside, Brett's already got all of the mattresses out and is blowing them up. I was so happy last Sunday; about ten o'clock Sunday morning, Gilea and Heather showed up, helped us get the mattresses put away, then split the sheets up between the three of us, and they each took a bundle home to wash. That made my week much, much easier. I told them they didn't have to do that, but Heather said, "You let us use your house every week. It's the least we can do." God, I love those girls.

Promptly at seven, the door opens and Joe and Belinda come in. Belinda's got something in a tote and she brings it into the kitchen and plops it down on the counter. "What's that?" I ask her.

"Something fun!" She pulls out three huge bottles of something clear.

"What is it?"

"It's flavored lube! Can you believe it? We got these big bottles at the office. We're supposed to pour it up in little bottles they sent with the big ones and hand them out as samples, but Dr. Coleman said she didn't want 'that vile stuff' in her office and told me to throw it away. No way would I do that! Besides, she's an awful prude to be a gynecologist."

"Oh my god! This stuff is so cool!" There's so much of it that it's bound to last us a month or two. The bottles are damn near a gallon apiece, and it had to be ridiculously expensive. That was quite the score.

Everybody shows up in a knot about that time. Hugs and kisses go all around, and then somebody says, "There they are!" Everybody steps aside as David and Holly walk in, and there are more hugs and kisses and tears.

"I want you two to know, Karen was crying last week because she missed you," Daniel tells both of them.

"No! Really?" Holly cries out and gets all teary-eyed.

"He's not lying," I say, and then I start crying even though I'm trying hard not to. David crosses the room and hugs me to him. He's sweet, always has been. He's not a really remarkable-looking guy, but he's cute, with a headful of dishwater blond hair and beautiful hazel eyes. Holly's tall and willowy, her skin as pale as Juan's is dark, and that red hair – gorgeous.

"I want you all to know how much we love you and appreciate you. No one could have lovers and friends who are as wonderful as you guys." David rubs my back as he hugs me, then takes my shoulders and pushes me back so he can look into my face and kiss me.

"So the job? How's that?" Brett asks.

Daniel interrupts. "My regional has thanked me three times already for hiring this guy. Just his first week, and he's already implemented some cost-saving measures that'll make a real difference. He's in line for a bonus his very first quarter with us – that's *never* happened before in the company's history. There's only one thing that's upsetting me." Daniel stops and looks around the room. "Don't – and I mean *don't* – any of you ever let things get as far into the dumper as these two did before they said something to someone. Come to the group and let us know. That's what we're here for. We're all lovers and friends, and lovers and friends take care of each other." Everyone in the group nods.

"Well, I want to say right here in front of everybody that I don't know who it was, but somebody paid up our house payments so we're out of trouble with the mortgage company. We really, really appreciate it. I wish whichever one of you it was would tell us so we could try to repay you." David is getting misty-eyed, but I know – every couple in the group had paid one of their missed house payments, so it was all of us.

"Not gonna happen. Just assume it was everyone, because we all love you. And we missed you last week. So let's get to it and make up for lost time!" Juan announces. He has his shirt off in a flash, and Belinda is already out of her top and bra. In less than a minute, we all have our clothes off and everybody is past ready.

Then Joe says, "You guys weren't here last week, and we *all* missed you. Both of you get picking choice – choose who and what and we'll indulge you. What'll it be?"

David gets a sly look on his face. He points at me. "I hear you had quite a time last week," he grins. I can't help but smile when I remember. "Holly and I want to ramp it up, take it to the next level."

A huge smile breaks out across Joe's face. "What've you got in mind?"

David points at Holly. "We want a couple of you to DP her. But there's more." Everybody waits. "I want the guy in her ass to let me fuck his ass. Anybody?"

To my surprise, Carson speaks up. "I'm in. I don't mind getting it from both directions." That was a revelation to me – a good one.

"Good deal." David stops, then says, "And we want somebody to face fuck her while they're penetrating her." He waits.

Finally, Juan says, "I'll fuck her mouth. Pussy?"

Brett raises his hand. "Be glad to. Thought maybe I'd do Karen this week, but this will be great."

Holly is almost bouncing up and down. "Ooooo, let's go for it! I can't wait!"

Brett plops himself down on a mattress. "Come mount me, beautiful." Holly trots across the room and climbs right up onto him. I watch as she lowers herself on my husband's cock and I'm so proud and happy to see her enjoy him so much. "Now put your forearms on my chest and arch your back. Carson, get on up here, buddy."

"Brett, stroke into her a couple of times while I get real good and hard." Carson is stroking his shaft methodically, and seeing him get harder and harder is a marvelous thing. Brett had already started moving in and out of her, and she's purring and smiling down at him, then she leans in and kisses him, and I watch as he runs his tongue in between her lips. When he sees Carson come up behind her, he says, "Arch it, honey. He's coming in."

I hear Belinda chime in, "Hey, here's the new lube." She pumps a big dollop into Carson's palm, and he coats his condom with it, then runs two slippery fingers into Holly's back door. The moan she lets out makes the room vibrate, and I look over at Angela – pussy nectar is already running down the inside of her leg. I look at Joe and throw my eyes toward Angela, and when he sees what I'm seeing, he walks over to her, whispers something to her, and takes her to a mattress. In seconds, he has her legs over his forearms and has lifted her ass into the air. The pounding he's giving her makes my knees weak, so I turn back to watch Holly and the guys.

By that time, Carson is buried in Holly's ass and has started stroking. Juan takes his place at Brett's side, and Holly leans out just enough to let him push his cock into her open mouth. The look on her face is pure bliss as the three men fill her from every direction, and I'm so jealous, but in a good way. In the meantime, David has slicked up his wrapped rod and he's gotten into place behind Carson. As Carson strokes into Holly's ass, he asks David, "So how do you want this to go?"

"You stroke into her, then back yourself onto me. Think that'll work?"

"Hell yeah, I think so. Let's try it." Carson pushes into Holly. When he's in up to his balls, he tells David, "Okay, put the head in my ass." I watch as David puts the head of his beautiful cock into Carson's tightness and waits while Carson begins his retreat from Holly and pushes himself back over David. He goes slowly, but once he has backed completely onto David, he strokes back into Holly and they begin the actual exchange. And as he backs out of Holly, Brett presses inward, filling her pussy from below. Every time Brett strokes into her pussy, Juan strokes into her throat.

The rest of us, with the exception of Joe and Angela, who are fucking like a frat boy and his little sis, watch in amazement and lust. Holly is so full and stretched so tight that she's moaning around Juan's dick, and all four men are groaning with optimum satisfaction. "Fuck me, this is good," Carson murmurs, and I go wet to the point of dripping.

Brett's hands go straight to Holly's tits. He works her nipples with crazy twisting and pulling, and she's wriggling almost like she's trying to get away from his fingers, which, by the way, are magical. That only makes him work at it harder, and she would be crying out, but Juan's dick down her throat keeps her from being able to make much noise at all. And David is so overcome that Daniel moves in behind him, puts his arms around the younger man's waist, and helps him stay upright instead of just collapsing into an overwhelmed puddle.

I've started playing with myself – I just can't help it. It's just so damned erotic that I have to do *something*. Angela and Joe have finished, and she gets down on her knees in front of me, takes my hands, and buries her mouth in my slit. I groan out and hold onto her hands. I hear Gilea say, "Karen, spread your legs out," and when I do, she scoots under me between my legs and buries her face in Angela's mound. Apparently Gilea tugs really hard on Angela's clit, because she sucks my nub in between her lips, which makes me almost collapse.

Katie is watching in slack-jawed amazement. I can tell this is well beyond her comprehension level. Then her face lights up when she feels a pair of hands come from behind her and grasp her breasts, and she turns and smiles at Joe when he leans down to her and sucks a nipple into his mouth, then pinches it between his teeth. Katie's nipples are unlike anyone else's in the group – they're large and soft, like oversized adolescent buds. They never really get hard, and the guys love to play with them and pretend that she's a twelve- or thirteen-year-old virgin. She even has a habit of playing the part, saying things like, "I've never done this before. Will it hurt?" or "I'm gonna be in so much trouble if my mom finds out." One night I even saw her play-fighting against Juan when he tried to hold her down and fuck her, and I heard her tell him, "No! No! I'm a virgin! Please, please don't hurt me!" His eyes lit up and he tore into her like a wild animal. But tonight, she goes to a mattress on all fours, drops her forearms to the mattress, and arches her back, sending her ass high into the air so her pussy is completely and totally exposed, and Joe buries himself in her in an instant and strokes with crazed abandon. In less than two minutes she's crying out and yelling, "Oh, god, Joe, fuck me good!"

Angela doubles her efforts, and I come with a shout and my knees almost buckle; she comes right behind me, courtesy of Gilea. Then we hear it.

Juan starts to moan, "Oh my god, I'm gonna come. Suck me, baby, keep sucking. Swallow hard, sweetheart." When he starts that, everyone's chiming in.

Brett says, "Sweet mother of god, you're tight, little one. Carson, I'm gonna start pumping." Then he starts fucking her with complete disregard for the rhythm Carson's keeping.

That's when Carson loses it. He starts slamming into Holly, then backing wildly onto David, who's started moaning and crying out, "Oh my god, tight, tight, tight! Fuck me, Carson! Oh shit, I'm coming!" He stiffens and unloads into his condom. When he does, Carson lets out a yell and buries himself in Holly, then holds still while David leans in, his cock filling Carson from behind, and David grinds into him a couple of times to finish off. That's enough for Juan, who unloads into Holly's mouth until his essence runs out of the corners of her lips, and seeing it running down her chin and on down her neck makes Brett stiffen and cry out. We watch his back arch as he drives his cock into her pussy one last time and then goes limp.

And poor Holly – she'd come five minutes earlier and hadn't been able to get away, so she's been convulsing the whole time, and she looks like she's going to pass out. As soon as Juan has his dick out of her mouth, she collapses on Brett's chest, and he wraps his arms around her and kisses the top of her head.

David manages to pull himself out of Carson, who then manages to pull himself out of Holly – she'd been buried under men. "You okay?" Brett asks Holly.

"Hell, every hole on my body hurts," we hear her say, then she giggles, "but they hurt good!" That makes Carson laugh, and David starts laughing too.

"Oh my god, that was good," Juan gasps, sitting down hard on the floor.

"Well, I guess you could tell that we all missed you last week!" Gilea starts laughing. That gets it started, and pretty soon everybody is laughing, just like always, and it feels good.

We get it under control just in time to hear Katie scream, "Oh, Joe, damn, you're a good fuck! I'm coming, I'm coming!" She stiffens under him and, when she does, he grinds into her and groans at the top of his lungs as he floods her cunt. When he stops panting, he turns and looks at the group.

"I don't know what the rest of you plan to do, but I made my contribution to the baby-making fund already!" Everybody really starts laughing then, and David and Holly look completely confused.

"Don't worry," Joe adds, "we'll explain to you two later."

That's when I notice Josh and Heather – they're over to the side on a mattress, and they're having some kind of serious discussion while they fuck each other. He kisses her long and deep, and they both come slowly and gently, rocking together. I'm watching them, and they're so beautiful, him sitting up with his legs wrapped under her ass, her sitting facing him with her legs around him and his shaft buried in her. They're sitting with one side to us, so I get to watch Heather's tits bounce every time she falls back onto his hardness. Someone else notices I'm watching and starts watching too. Pretty soon, all eyes are on them. Finally, Brett asks, "What's with you two?"

Josh turns to the group and smiles. "This is the five year anniversary of the first time I took her. Every year on this date, at seven thirty, no matter what we're doing, we stop and make love, even if we have to do it in a public place or leave a meeting or something. It's just what we do to celebrate our physical union."

There's a chorus of "Awwww!" from the women in the group. "How sweet!" Angela says. "I remember our first time." She turns to Juan and he winks at her.

My mind goes back to the first time Brett and I had each other. I was with a couple of friends at a bar and one of them spotted him. She finally went up to the bar and talked to him, then went out the back door on his arm. Ten minutes later, she came in and told our other friend that he wanted to talk to her, but she didn't give an explanation as to what they'd been out there doing. So our other friend strolled up to the bar to talk to him, and they disappeared out the back door too. Ten minutes later, and still with no explanation, she came back in and told me that he wanted to talk to me. I was too curious to say no. When I got to the bar, I looked him up and down, and he did the same to me. And he just straight-up said, "I guess you're wondering what your friends and I were doing out back."

"Yes, that question had crossed my mind."

Then he said, "I took them out back and fucked them. I wanted to see which of the three of you was the best fuck. You game?" *Hell yeah,* I thought, *bring it on!* He led me out the back door, threw me up against the wall, ripped my lacy underthings down, and fucked the hell out of me right there. It was breathtaking – *he* was breathtaking. When he finished with me, he pointed down the alley as I pulled up my panties and tried to straighten myself up. "See that Ferrari down there?"

"Yeah?" I panted.

He laughed. "I really brought them out here to show them the car. You were the only one of the three of you that I wanted to fuck. And you're every bit as good as I dreamed." Then he leaned in and kissed me, a deep, hot kiss that made me pant even harder, followed by, "Go tell your friends that you're going home with me and get back out here." I couldn't run fast enough. When I came out the back door, he had the car running and was waiting for me; I hopped in and he took off. We went straight to his apartment and fucked all night long.

And we've been together ever since. Twenty-two years. I'd say that's a pretty good run. And every time he looks at me with those blue eyes, I get wet. I can't help it. We've kept it fresh and fun, and watching him fuck the women in our group really gets me excited. So I have no reason to think that will ever change, that wanting him, needing him thing.

So I'm standing here reminiscing, watching Heather and Josh, and I feel someone behind me. I know the touch well. "Thinking back?" Brett asks and smiles.

"I sure am, lover." I kiss the tip of his nose and he comes back with a kiss on my mouth, his tongue slipping between my lips and tickling mine. Then he slips a finger into my pussy and I can't help it – my back arches and I press against him. He laughs, takes it out, and kisses me again.

He points toward the door. "I think everybody is ready to go home. Wanna steer them all in that direction?"

"Sure. Most of them." Actually, I'm thinking about something different. "There's something I want, if it's okay with you." I whisper to him and he nods and smiles.

I make it over to Belinda and it looks like I'm hugging her, but I whisper in her ear, "You guys hang back, okay?" When I turn her loose, her whole face is lit up and she nods.

When everyone else is gone except for Belinda and Joe, I turn to Brett and he asks them, "Will you guys stay the night with us again? We'd love to take this to the bedroom."

Joe slips his arms around my waist. "If you'll strip right here, right this minute." I start shucking off my jeans. Apparently Brett's said the same thing to Belinda, because she can't get out of her clothes fast enough either. "Now, you know what we want. Nice and slow."

I pull one of the air mattresses to the middle of the room, and Belinda and I climb onto it. I look at her, grin, and head down to her slit, tonguing it as soon as I get there. Once I'm between her legs and comfortable, I go down on her properly and watch her squirm and groan. I hear a moan and check the sofa; Joe and Brett both are watching us and stroking themselves, and I love seeing that, their hands wrapped around their own shafts. Suddenly, I need something in my honey hole desperately. I get Belinda off and then she works on me, but I still want a cock in there. I'm aching for it.

When I come, both of the guys finally shoot. Then Brett gets up and leaves the room. When he comes back, he's got a box, and I don't remember ever seeing it before. He opens it and takes something out; two somethings, actually.

Butt plugs. Big ones. They take one apiece, lube the monsters up, and slip them into both of us. They're so damn big that I have trouble taking it, but he manages to get it in there. Before I can say anything about how it feels, Brett goes back into the box and brings out two more items.

They're the biggest, scariest dildos I've ever seen. Before I can stop myself, I blurt out, "I don't think you can get that thing in me." Wrong thing to say, because now they're both determined to do just that. Belinda glances over at me, and I can see that she's already getting a little panicky. To try to calm her down, I smile at her. I mean, if they won't fit in, they won't fit in. End of discussion.

"Oh, we're not just planning to get them in there. We're planning to fuck you with them," Brett announces.

Joe takes one of the big bottles of lube and slathers down the purple dildo. Brett's got the red one in his hand, and he does the same. They look at each other and grin, then Joe comes to me and Brett goes to Belinda. Joe looks at Brett again with a smirk and says, "This isn't my pussy, so if I tear it up, it doesn't matter to me."

Brett laughs and says, "I was just thinking the exact same thing. Split 'em open, I say!" he shouts in his best medieval voice. I almost giggle, then I remember what they're about to do, and I hold onto that giggle. I might need it later.

"Let's see who can get it all the way in first," Joe tells Brett. "You do the countdown."

"Okay, here goes. Three ... two ... one," and I feel the tip press against my sex. Until that moment I'd thought they were messing with us.

They weren't.

Joe growls at me, "Spread 'em, baby, far as they'll go." I bring my knees up and out, and I feel him press harder. There's a tiny little burn. He keeps going. I feel my cunt start to open up a little, but not enough. That's when he draws it back and then shoves it – considerably.

I see fireworks, and not the good kind, more like the kind where somebody dropped a match in a gunpowder factory. And I can feel the head of that thing about to breech my entrance. By this time, I'm panting and shaking. I remember my training for fisting and I bear down like I'm giving birth. It hurts like a motherfucker. And then I feel the "pop" of the head of the thing snapping into my pussy. Belinda's having lots more difficulty with it, and Brett says to Joe, "What do you do to her to make her open up?"

"Never had that problem before. Must be your technique!" Joe laughs. He's got the first four inches of the purple fence post in me, and I don't know how much more I can take.

I watch Brett, and I see him do something I hadn't thought of: He puts a finger on either side of the head of the red monster, presses his fingers into Belinda, then uses them to stretch her open while he pushes the dildo into her. She cries out, but I look over and see the entire head slip inside her cunt. Now it's game on for Brett. He's trying to make up for lost time by shoving it into her faster, and she's crying out, screaming actually.

But I've got my own problems in my own downtown block. I look down to see Joe shove another two inches into me, and I realize the damn thing is over halfway into my box. The stretch is excruciating, but I want it. I check to see how Belinda's faring, and Brett's already got the thing more than halfway into her. She's broken out in a sweat. And I'm headed in the right direction.

Five minutes later, I look down. I'm surprised to see that the entire purple thing is buried in me, right up to its latex balls. Joe leans down to my ear and whispers, "We'll let them sit for a few minutes, give your pussy time to adjust. Then we'll fuck you." He starts kissing me and tweaking my nipples.

I don't think I'll ever adjust to that thing but, in about two minutes, I feel my walls start to soften and form themselves to the dildo. *I can do this,* I think. *It's not as bad as I thought it would be.* I see that the red one is firmly buried in Belinda, and she stares down at it, then over to me. She's starting to look not quite so panicky.

Just as I think I've got it under control, Joe takes a hand from my nipple and starts to stroke my clit. The idea of coming with this thing in me is more than I can wrap my brain around. I'm so stretched out that there's no way my pussy can contract around the giant toy, not to mention the butt plug, so I don't know exactly what will happen. I see that Brett's doing the exact same thing to Belinda, and now there's full-blown terror on her face. I find myself wishing they'd restrained our hands, because I don't know what I'm going to do when the orgasm hits.

And then it does. I feel myself slip off the edge and it knots my belly, my poor pussy stretched so far around the big log that it can't spasm, and the sensation snatches the breath right out of my lungs. I see exploding balls of fire, lightning bolts, and I'm pretty sure that was my dead English teacher, all dancing behind my lids. I start to scream and I can't even get it out – it's trapped in my throat, my whole body rocking since my pussy and ass can't tighten. As I shriek, I hear Belinda do the same, screaming expletives the likes of which I'm sure she learned in a Belgium brothel – I don't even know what some of them mean. And Joe doesn't let up. He keeps stroking and stroking, watching my stomach muscles ripple, and I see that he's looking at the outline of the huge dildo under the flesh of my belly. It's plain as day; I can see it, and it makes me scream louder.

After what seems like two hours of this mind-altering misery, Joe finally stops touching my clit. I breathe a sigh of relief. But I know what's next.

He slides the dildo out and shoves it back in. I scream. He does it again. I cry out. Once again, and I groan – loudly. By the fourth stroke, I'm moaning incoherently, and I know full well that I'm incoherent, but I don't seem to be able to do anything about it. He's pumping it into me rhythmically and my body is trying to adjust. I watch as Brett shoves the red one into Belinda with a considerable amount of force, and she almost comes up off the mattress, screaming and reaching for him, probably to claw his eyes out, but he manages to stay just out of her grasp.

Joe keeps pumping it in and out of me, occasionally taking a different angle. When he finds what I assume he thinks is the right one, he shoves the dildo into me and I shake and scream out, "Oh fuck!" Then he *really* picks up the pace.

That's when I realize I'm actually being fucked by the biggest damn dildo I've ever seen. Joe looks very pleased with himself as he watches it go in and out of my cunt. The angle he's taken makes the damn thing rub against my G-spot, and I'm completely and totally overwhelmed with the sensations, the friction of the dildo's ribs, the burn of the stretch, the pressure of it slamming into the end of my channel, the swelling I can feel my clit doing just from the arousal, not to mention the fact that this dildo's as big around as a Gala apple and at least fourteen inches long; well, that's probably an exaggeration, but that's how it looks and feels to me. I have to wonder what kind of long-term damage this will cause, but it's done now, and I just try to find some enjoyment in it all.

I'm so tensed up that I can't come, so Joe just keeps going. He and Brett have already high-fived each other, and they're laughing and comparing notes, god bless 'em, while Belinda and I try to stay sane. She's gotten quiet, and I'm getting sort of worried about her, but I can't even speak to ask her if she's okay; I can't do anything but lie there and take it. Time kind of stands still as it goes on and on, and I realize after awhile that it's not so bad. Another five minutes, and I start to moan and my hips begin to rock. I hear Joe tell Brett, "Hey, look! She's getting into it!"

"She is too!" Brett laughs. I check on Belinda and find her twisting and pulling her nipples in some kind of state of absent-mindedness, her hips thrusting with every inward stroke. To my horror, Brett fishes his phone out of his jeans pocket and begins to make a video of what he's doing to Belinda.

"No!" I start yelling. Then I notice that Joe's doing the exact same thing to me, and I start to scream, "No! Stop! Don't do that!"

"Baby, we're not getting your faces, just your tits and everything below. We want to watch this later; we want you two to watch it later. Hell, we want the whole group to watch it. It's just amazing. So damn hot," Joe murmurs. Brett nods as he keeps filming and shoving the dildo in and out of Belinda. "I don't know if I can hang onto the phone or not, but here goes."

Joe starts a purposeful ramming, then picks up the pace. He's running the thing in and out of me so fast that it's almost burning my skin, and then it happens: I come. My whole body clamps down and

I bow inward in the middle, shaking and moaning through clenched teeth and, as I look downward, I can clearly see the outline of the dildo under the muscles of my belly. He keeps going, faster and faster, and I can't stop, can't get any relief. Suddenly, he stops with the thing buried to the hilt in me, and I just collapse.

It takes me a little while, but I turn my head to look at Belinda and see Brett speed stroking the red dildo in and out of her. I watch her come, her body stiffen, her eyes roll back. She screams for what seems like a full five minutes, during which Brett will not let up. Her head lolls to the side and, when it does, Brett stops just like Joe did, the latex balls of the monster against Belinda's labial lips. Out of curiosity, I try to clench my vaginal muscles and find I can't – they're too stretched over the shaft. It would be nice to say that everything was numb, but it wasn't. It was more hyper-sensitive than anything, and I was miserable.

Joe leans down and kisses my clit, which makes my exhausted hips buck against my will. "I'll take it out now, angel," he laughs, then pulls it out slowly. The burn doesn't go away; it's still burning, and I get the feeling it will for days. I hear Belinda shriek as Brett pulls the red one out of her.

"Oh, god, what now?" I moan. Instead of answering me, Joe starts to stroke my clit again, and I almost scream. Everything is swollen, everything is over-sensitized, and it takes under two minutes for me to roll screaming into an orgasm, all points below my waist constricting and throbbing, and I know Brett's doing the exact same thing to Belinda.

When Joe finally stops and my muscles relax, he climbs up beside me and takes me in his arms. And just as I think any tenderness he slips to me will be misplaced, he looks me in the eye and says, "Oh my god, baby, that was the damn sexiest thing I've ever seen. You made me so hard that I'm aching, and I'm gonna fuck you right now. And it'll be okay, really." I really doubt that, but he climbs on top of me and slips his cock into me, and it feels like it always does. I hear Belinda murmur, "Oh, god, Brett, that feels so good," and I know he's pumping her. The human body is a miraculous thing.

When they're done with us, Brett picks me up, Joe picks Belinda up, and they carry both of us to the bedroom. Brett and Joe get a warm washcloth apiece, and they spread our legs wide and wipe us down. The warmth of the washcloth feels good to my sore pussy, and I'm surprised to find that I'm getting drowsy. When Brett climbs into the bed with us and wraps me up in his arms, I snuggle into his chest and sigh deeply.

"God, baby, I love you so much," he whispers to me. "I hope you're not mad at the way we played with you."

I think for a few seconds, and then I giggle. "I've always been a slut, so I guess you can do anything you want to me and I'll stick around!" I look up into his eyes and find them smiling back at me.

"That's what a man dreams of – a slut who'll let me do anything to her, fuck anybody I want her to fuck, let me fuck anybody I want to fuck, and still love me and come home to only me. I've got the greatest life on earth." He kisses the top of my head and whispers, "Go to sleep, precious. If anyone ever earned a rest, you two girls did."

Belinda and Joe get up before it gets light and go home, hoping that our nosiest neighbor doesn't see them, and we get kisses and hugs from them before they go. After they leave, I fall back to sleep on Brett's chest, listening to his peaceful, even breathing. He's wrong; *I've* got the greatest life on earth. I've got seven gorgeous guys to fuck me unconscious, six beautiful women to play with me, and more love than anyone could imagine. We'll always be closer to Joe and Belinda – after all, they were our firsts – but I love them all, and they love me.

Brett was right: Any baby this group brings into the world will be the most loved child in the universe, hands down.

CHAPTER FIVE

Gloria

They think I didn't see them, but I did. I saw that couple sneak out of Brett and Karen's house this morning in the dark. Everyone else left last night, but they stayed. I'd love to know what they were doing in there.

I tried to look in the windows, but they had those blinds pulled down tight. I could hear something, though. It was mostly a lot of screaming and swearing. But there weren't any noises like someone being beaten, so I didn't know what to do.

At breakfast I tell Russell, "I'm beginning to think those Brett and Karen people are some kind of perverts."

"Oh? Why's that?"

"Because of all those people coming over every week. And that couple who went home in the dark this morning," I tell him.

"Did it ever occur to you," he says, looking over the top of the newspaper, "that maybe they were watching a movie and fell asleep? And when they woke up they decided they should go on home? And there are lots of other possibilities too. So don't go jumping to conclusions." Then he goes back to the newspaper.

"Doesn't anyone else in this neighborhood care about what's going on? About our property values?" I can't believe he's just dismissing this – it's very serious.

"Property values? Unless they're having sex out on the lawn, they're not hurting anyone."

"That'll probably be next!" I shout at him. "And I don't want to have to watch that!"

"Oh, hell, woman, you'd be the first in line with your binoculars!" he tells me.

I swear, I'm beginning to wonder if my husband is some kind of pervert too. My nerves are shot. I think I'll make myself a Bloody Mary. I love tomato juice.

CHAPTER SIX

Karen

I can't help but smile when I hear Daniel say, "Hey, take it easy on her! Remember?"

"Yeah, the baby you hurt could be mine!" Joe chimes in.

"Oh, yeah, sorry. Don't want to hurt the little guy," David says.

"It's okay. He's just overprotective. Do me good, sweetie. I need a serious fucking. He acts like I'm made of china," Katie grins. "Just don't lean right on my belly," she tells him, rubbing her roundness gently like she was stroking a pet.

"He's just as bad," Angela says, pointing at Juan. Josh is getting ready to drill away into her. He came in and made a big deal of announcing that he'd like to fuck a pregnant woman because they might want a baby someday. Angela's not quite as far along as Katie, so there's really no danger unless the two of them get crazy. And it's been known to happen.

We've gotten started without Carson and Gilea. I don't know where they are; when I talked to Carson last night, he said they were coming.

I hear a key in the lock, and Carson unlocks the door and holds it for Gilea, who waves at everyone, kisses Daniel and Belinda on her path to the bathroom, and disappears behind the door. "Too much water?" I ask Carson.

"Something like that." He turns and sees Katie, and he smiles and kisses her while David fucks her. When he looks into her eyes, she nods, and he puts his hand on her belly and feels it, then kisses it. When his lips touch it, there's a moving lump that meets them and he yells out, "Hey! He kicked me! You shouldn't do that," he says, pointing at her belly with mock sternness. "I just might be your daddy."

He shucks his clothes, then makes a trip across the room and kisses me deeply. "Hey, beautiful!" he grins at me.

"Hey yourself!" I giggle. Carson and I had an extremely intense session last week, and I'm still glowing from it. He drops to his knees, opens my slit with his fingers, and his tongue finds my swollen nub and starts to circle it slowly. I moan and brace myself with my hands on his shoulders. I'm just starting to fall into it when I hear a shriek and the bathroom door bursts open.

"LOOK!" Gilea holds up something, and it takes me a minute to figure out what it is.

It's a pregnancy test. And it's positive.

Carson makes it to her first and sweeps her up in his arms, giving her a long, deep kiss, then looking into her eyes and saying loudly enough so the whole group can hear, "I love you more than anything on earth, do you know that, beautiful?" Then he surprises us when he starts to cry.

Within seconds there's a knot of twelve other people crowded around them, kissing them, hugging them, congratulating them. Over the din I hear Joe say, "Damn, I love breastfeeding. It's gonna be an all-you-can-eat buffet in here!"

Then I hear Brett say, "Damn is right. This is going to get expensive with seven guys to pass out cigars for three babies!" Somebody laughs.

I look around and I can't help but think that we've *all* got the greatest lives in the world. We're so lucky to have each other. I can't wait to hold those babies. They're going to be the happiest kids ever.

CHAPTER SEVEN

Gloria

"So how many pregnant friends do you have?" I can't tell how many of them there are coming and going anymore.

"Three of them are pregnant now. We're all really excited. I get to be an auntie!" That's the most animated I've ever seen Karen Reynolds. It's almost like she's having a baby herself.

"That's really nice! I hope I get to see the babies sometime," I tell her, and I really mean it.

"I'm sure you will. I have every intention of babysitting." She's practically gushing. I really don't know what to make of it, all this enthusiasm about other people's babies. I'm about halfway expecting to get a baby shower invitation – for her.

They really must all be very good friends.

CHAPTER EIGHT

Karen

"I was thinking... Do we all consider ourselves committed to each other?" Angela has posed this question to the group, and everyone is trying to figure out where this is going.

There's a murmur around the room. I think most everybody is surprised that she'd even ask that. My Brett was the first one to answer.

"I'm committed to every one of you. Every last one," Brett says. "And I don't mind anyone knowing."

"Me too," Joe answers. Everyone is nodding. "Belinda?"

"Absolutely." She nods too. "If I were to have sex with someone outside this group, I'd feel like I were cheating on all of you. Every one." Gilea and Katie nod in agreement.

"I feel the exact same way," Daniel chimes in. "Is there anyone here who doesn't feel that way?"

Everyone who hasn't spoken is shaking their head. I look around. These are my lovers. I'm married to Brett, but these people? They're my spouses almost as surely as he is.

"So here's my idea. Why don't we do a big commitment ceremony? You know, like a marriage ceremony? Where we all commit to each other?"

It's quiet, and then Carson says, "I'm for it. Absolutely."

"Me too," Daniel adds. "I think that would be great. Could we do it here?" They all look at me.

"I don't see why not. Does anyone know someone who might be willing to officiate?" I ask.

Joe gives us all a wide grin. "I sure do! Belinda, do you still have James' number?"

At the mention of his name, Angela, Juan, Brett, and I all have to smile. The thought of James and Marcia coming for a commitment ceremony is past wonderful. The rest don't know them – it was before their time with us – but the six of us have missed them terribly.

"I can barely wait!" Angela gushes. "Can we start planning?"

"Oh, lets!" Holly cries out, then she blushes. "I want to belong with all of you."

"Honey, it's too late." Joe's voice is all smooth, warm honey and his smile is bright. "You guys already do."

It was decided that all of the ladies are wearing red, and we look stunning, The guys look just a good as we do, all decked out in gray. And we got a surprise: Carson and Gilea had never made it legal, so they want to actually do the deed. Good thing James can legally marry couples in our state. Gilea wants to wear white, and no one has a problem with that!

When James and Marcia walk in, we all surround them and lavish them with hugs and kisses. They live on the other end of the state now, and that's a good five and a half hours away, so it's rare that we get to see them. I can't speak for everyone else, but I miss them almost too much. And they're staying the night with us, so Juan, Angela, Joe, and Belinda were asked to stay too. The eight of us have a whole evening together to screw each other's brains out. I'm so excited!

James has us all stand in a circle, holding hands. As usual, we stand beside whomever we're married to, but James says, "No. Each woman should be between two men to whom she's not legally wed. Carson and Gilea should stand in the middle." I get it, and I cross the circle and stand between David and Juan. Everyone else shifts around, and the ceremony begins.

James has written vows for all of us to repeat, and I love it all. We promise to love each other and take care of each other. He has special vows for Carson and Gilea, regular wedding vows, and then includes them in our joint vows. It's a beautiful ceremony, and I don't think there's a dry eye in the group.

As we're finishing up, I see something move out of the corner of my eye, somewhere around the gate. Our privacy fence is tall, but there are gaps in the boards, and I could swear I see someone standing out there looking in. If there is someone out there, well, I know exactly who it is.

CHAPTER NINE

Gloria

There are cars everywhere; I recognize them from the parties. But there was a couple going in that I've never seen before, and he's all dressed up like a preacher. I just want to see what's going on.

So I've decided to sneak over there and see if I can get a glimpse of what they're doing. Those fence boards are far enough apart that I should be able to see in the back yard. That seems to be where they are.

I can just barely see them. A bunch of the women are wearing red, and one is in white. A wedding? Why would anybody wear red to a wedding? That's just weird.

I'm trying to hear, but it's hard. Something about commitments to each other. But it doesn't sound like he's talking about just two people. I'm not sure. There's something really, really fishy about this "wedding."

So the couple in the middle kiss and everyone cheers. How sweet! That lady is really pretty; she's kind of round and soft, but really pretty. And her dress is pretty too. And then something really weird happens.

All of the guys get into a circle, with the women on the inside, and each woman goes to a man, kisses him, and then goes to the next. They kiss every man in the circle. And this ain't no soft little peck, no sir. This is a real tongue-down-the-throat kind of kiss, the kind you do right before you have you-know-what. What the hell are they doing? Then the other couple, the one that the guy looks like a preacher? They get in the circle and everybody kisses them that same way. Oh my god – now the women are kissing *each other!* What the hell . . .

I don't know what to think. It's disgusting. I can't believe I'm seeing this. Are they some kind of perverts or something? Just wait until I tell Russell. He'll have a fit and want them run out of the neighborhood. We don't need this kind of thing here. We're all good, law-abiding, clean, nice people. We don't need that filth around here. I need a margarita. It's going to take me all afternoon to calm down after this.

CHAPTER TEN

Karen

The reception is heavenly. Every woman in the group made her favorite dessert, and we're all stuffed. I have two cases of wine that I had shipped in, and I think that'll be fine. We've got three pregnant women in the group and they won't be drinking, so that means there'll be plenty for all of us.

Gilea looks so cute in her wedding dress. She's not showing yet, but she will be soon.

Angela and Katie are round as plums. As I watch, every man in the group, at some point, walks up behind a pregnant woman, whispers something in her ear, and wraps his arms around her waist to rub her belly. It's precious. Makes me wish I were . . . nah. Three babies is enough for this group.

When we've had our fill of cake, cookies, and punch, and I use the word "punch" liberally, we all start to get really animated. We're going on a honeymoon! All sixteen of us! Yeah, James and Marcia took the weekend off to go with us, and we're all really excited. It's been years since I've fucked James, and I still remember how good he is. And I can tell Joe is really excited to see Marcia again. When it was just the eight of us, we all loved to watch Joe and Marcia go at it. They were poetry in bed, almost like their sex was choreographed. Those were good times, Juan, Angela, Joe, Belinda, James, Marcia, Brett, and me. It seems like so long ago, and yet they're standing here and it feels like just yesterday. James laughs loudly when he asks, "So who's the father of these three?" pointing at the pregnant girls, and all of the men in the room except for him raise their hands.

I can see right now, it's going to be hard to wait until we get to the honeymoon. And before I can get back to the living room, James has grabbed me around the waist, pulled me into the laundry room, and pushed my skirt up around my waist. I'm appropriately bare, except for a garter belt and red stockings that match my dress.

"God, I've missed all of you," James whispers into my neck.

"We've missed you too," I whisper back. "Got some of that spectacular cock for me? I've missed it so much."

"Yes ma'am, it's all yours for the moment. I don't think anybody's going to be able to wait until we get to the resort." We've booked a suite at a resort at the beach, and I'm itching to get there, but right now I'm itching for James. "Take a look out there."

And he's right – it's on. Joe's got Marcia on the dining room table and everyone is watching and smiling. As he powers into her, I hear him murmur, "Damn, woman, your pussy is as fine as I remember!" Her head's hanging down over the edge of the table and Carson's fucking down into her throat like a steam engine. They'd never met before, but they have now.

"Forget them. Fuck me like you mean it. I've missed you." I gasp as he impales me on that big shaft of his, and realize I'd forgotten how hard and hot he can be. "God, James, I think you've gotten better with age!"

He laughs. "I could say the same for you! I love that you girls know exactly what you want and don't mind asking for it. It's a real turn-on. You know, we've got to get together more often. I know we're over five hours apart, but that's not too far to go for a spectacular lay. And you, my dear, are spectacular." He slams into my cunt to the point of pain and kisses me long and deep. I feel myself melting into him. James is the reason that all of us are together. He was my first ménage and Marcia was Joe's. They brought us all in and made us a family.

"Shit, can't you guys wait?" I hear Brett say as he comes into the laundry room looking for a tea towel. But he's grinning as he says it, and when he catches a look at the expression on my face as Joe pumps me, he leans in, kisses me, and shuffles back into the living room. My guy. I love and trust him more than I thought possible, and he feels the same about me.

I feel my climax rising, a gnawing behind my clit, and I hear James say, "Oh, baby, I'm coming. Ready for me? 'Cause I'm sure ready for you."

Before I can nod the orgasm takes me, and I'm writhing against him. He keeps stroking into me until it's subsiding, and I feel his cock lengthen and stiffen even greater, then the warmth and wetness pours into me and drips down my leg. I want to suck him, want to lick his cum off my own leg, want him to fuck my ass until I'm screaming.

Wow. This is gonna be some honeymoon!

CHAPTER ELEVEN

Gloria

Those parties are still going on. Some of those women are pregnant, and you'd think they'd quit partying, but nooooo. They're still over there every week.

I told Russell what I'd seen through the fence. Know what he said? "Gloria, if I were those people, I'd have you arrested for trespassing and being a peeping tom. Leave them alone. So a pregnant woman got married. I would think you'd be happy about that so they're not living in sin." He just doesn't get it.

Thank goodness we've got some nice neighbors down the street. One day I asked Donna, Donna Millican, two doors down, who those couples were coming to their house. Know what she told me? "We're religious counselors. We do counseling for young couples who're having marital problems. You know, the bonds of marriage are blessed. There's just too much divorce these days, don't you think, Gloria?"

"Oh, indeed I do! It's sad, really." I shook my head and said, "I'm so glad we've got some neighbors of faith who help others in their time of need."

"Amen, sister. Now, we've got a couple coming in an hour, and I've got to get some cookies out for them, some fruit, and some of my granny's sweet tea. Bless you, honey, and we'll be praying for you and Russell."

"Thank you, dearie! We'll be praying for you too." She's so nice. Her husband, Connor, is such a nice guy, so attractive and clean-shaven. And the Hendersons, Greg and Becca, are pretty nice too. But sometimes I wonder what they're up to, especially since that sister of hers moved in with them.

AUTHOR'S NOTE

This book is the first of the Harper's Cove series. Join the neighborhood as Gloria does her best to find out what all of the neighbors are up to. You'll meet Karen and Brett, Donna and Connor, Becca and Greg, and more neighbors as they go about their business, all the while thinking they're the only neighbors on the cove who have a secret to keep.

As of publication, the number of future novellas is unknown, but expect six to nine of them. So keep reading and enjoy peeking into the lives of the neighbors of Harper's Cove!

ABOUT THE AUTHOR

Deanndra Hall lives in far western Kentucky with her partner of 30+ years and three crazy little dogs. She spent years writing advertising copy, marketing materials, educational texts, and business correspondence, and designing business forms and doing graphics design. After reading a very popular erotic romance book, her partner said, "You can write better than this!" She decided to try her hand at a novel. In the process, she fell in love with her funny, smart, loving, sexy characters and the things they got into, and the novel became a series.

Deanndra enjoys all kinds of music, kayaking, working out at the local gym, reading, and spending time with friends and family, as well as working in the fiber and textile arts. And chocolate's always high on her list of favorite things!

On the Web: www.deanndrahall.com

Email: DeanndraHall@gmail.com

Facebook: facebook.com/deanndra.hall

Twitter: twitter.com/DeanndraHall

Blog: deanndrahall.blogspot.com

Substance B: substance-b.com/DeanndraHall

Mailing address: P.O. Box 3722, Paducah, KY 42002-3722

Here's a sneak peek from some of the author's other titles . . .

From Laying a Foundation,
Book 1 in the
Love Under Construction Series

"I think everything is as ready as we can get it," Nikki told Tony as she stood in the kitchen on that evening, looking around.

"Then I guess I'll lock up and we'll call it a day," He shuffled off to lock the front door. Nikki turned to lock the back door, then turned off the kitchen lights. As she passed the island in the middle of the kitchen, a pair of strong hands grabbed her around the waist and lifted her onto the island.

"Yeesh! You scared the bejesus out . . ." she tried to say, but Tony covered her mouth with his and kissed her – hard. When he pulled back, she was breathless. "Wow, that was . . ." and he gave her a repeat performance, this time running both hands up under her top and peeling it off, then unbuttoning and unzipping her shorts. "You're . . ."

"Determined to have you. Right now. Want it? Say yes, baby," he murmured into her neck, then kissed her again, sucking her lower lip in between his.

"Yesssssss," she moaned, and he dug his fingers into her waist and picked her up. She promptly wrapped her legs around him, her arms clasped around his neck. They made it as far as the dining room table, biting each other's lips, tongues lashing into each other, before he sat her down on it, yanked her shorts off, then peeled off his tee and jeans. He climbed up onto the table with her and stared down at her in the darkness, his eyes intense, almost glowing.

"I should take you right here," he hissed into her ear, then bit her neck. Instead of making it easy for him, Nikki managed to wriggle away from him and took off running, giggling the whole time.

She made it as far as the foyer. Tony caught up with her, grabbed her around the waist, and spun her to look at him. "You're not getting away this time, little girl," he snarled at her. "I've got you and I'm not letting you go." This time, he reached around her and snapped the hooks of her bra loose, then locked his fingers into his boxer briefs, slid them down, and stepped out of them. Nikki purred when she got a glimpse of his cock, hard and waiting. He snatched her lacy hipsters off, then lifted her up again, and she wrapped her long, sculpted legs around his waist.

She wanted to kiss him again, long and slow, but before she could say or do anything, Tony wrapped his hands under her ass, lifted her a little higher, and impaled her on his rigid cock. Nikki stifled a scream as he bored into her pussy and showed no mercy, and Tony groaned and wedged her between his body and the wall, pistoning into her like a four-stroke engine as he held her there. He bit her neck again and, in turn, she bit his shoulder just like she'd done in the back of the SUV earlier in the day. He moaned into her ear, "I just wanna fuck you until I can't fuck you anymore. You are so goddamn sexy that you make me crazy for you."

"Then fuck me," she whispered back. "Fuck me hard. Just pound me until I scream for you to stop."

"Like I'd listen," he snickered and tied into her. His mouth found hers, and he kissed her so hard that she was sure he'd bruised her lips, then he latched onto her neck again and kissed, sucked, and bit it until she was nearly mad. He worked fast and hard, enjoying her cries against his collarbone, the pulses of her hot, wet sheath around his cock, and the hardness of her rigid peaks against his chest. He wished he could stop time or at least pause it, make a mental picture of them together, freeze the intensity of the sparks she gave off as her flint and his stone came together, as one's body burnished the other's to brilliance in that moment, so he could always recall it. Wanting to capture it all so he could enjoy it again later, sit in his office and think about it, picture her in his mind while he was at a jobsite, dream about her as she lay beside him sleeping in the night, he listened to her, soaked in the feel of her skin. He waited as long as he could before he poured himself into her in a gasping, moaning thrust that tuned her up until he was sure that Helene could hear them, even down at her house. Hell yeah, he hoped she could.

His possession of her body was too much for Nikki, and she tightened and came around him, screaming out, her fingers in his hair. When he stopped, she leaned in and locked her lips onto his, holding his face against hers until she couldn't breathe. "Sweet mother of god, babe, what's gotten into you today?" she panted when she finally broke the kiss.

"You. You're under my skin. Permanently. And I'm not complaining – not at all!" he laughed, then kissed her again. "I think it's about time I started living a more spontaneous life, stop planning everything out to the letter, start fucking you when I want, where I want, how I want, and making you want it too. And do you want it?" he asked with a seriousness that startled her.

"Want it? God, I crave it. Just cut loose!" she laughed back and kissed him.

"Let's go finish this in the bedroom," he told her as he carried her up the stairs. "I'll show you 'cut loose!'"

Thirty minutes later, she was still overwhelmed with his pressure inside her, his big, dark hands on her pale skin like molten lava, molded to her, pouring over her, twisting and pulling her nipples, flicking and stroking her clit. The sight of him above her drove her to the edge until his eyes closed and she saw that look on his face that said he was lost in ecstasy, lost in her. That look was all she needed; her own need consumed her and, as he buried himself in her over and over, she rasped her clit against his pelvis and came, repeating his name like a prayer. Within seconds, he groaned out his own climax. The liquid fire of his seed filled her, and she fell onto his chest, panting and moaning. His arms encircled her and tightened against her skin, and she'd never felt so desirable or so loved, so satisfied and so hungry for more.

"Are you trying to kill me?" she asked as he burrowed his face into her hair and kissed the top of her head.

"Yes. Death by sex," he chuckled as she licked his nipple.

"Correction: Death by great sex. Big difference," she giggled as he kissed the top of her head again. "But what a way to go!"

From Tearing Down Walls,
Book 2 in the
Love Under Construction Series

The club was starting to fill up, and the bar was busier than usual. Laura was drawing a couple of beers from a tap when she heard a woman at the bar say, "Holy shit, who's that? That's one extremely tall, dark, and hot Dom. Wonder if he's got a sub?" Laura turned to see who she was talking about and nearly fainted.

It was Vic Cabrizzi. And it was a Vic Cabrizzi she'd never seen before.

The mild-mannered man who'd sidled up to the bar and tried to make small talk with her was nowhere in this guy. Vic was six feet and eight inches of pure, dark, steaming sex in leather. He had the top half of his elbow-length black hair pulled up in a half-tail with a leather wrap, and his torso looked like it was trying to escape through the skin-tight black tee he was wearing. As he made his way toward the bar, the crowd parted to let him through as though they were in awe of the masculinity gliding across the room like a panther. Her eyes couldn't help but be drawn to his ass, and it looked especially fine under those leathers, not to mention the more-than-obvious bulge in the front of them. The room started to get spotty, and Laura realized she'd been holding her breath. *What the fuck?* was all she could get to run through her mind.

"Well! Guess by the look on your face that you approve of our newest service Dom!" Steve walked up to the bar and took a stool. Even in the dim lighting, Steve could see Laura's face turn three shades of red.

"Cabrizzi? Are you kidding?" she asked, incredulous. "You can't be serious!"

"Look at him, Laura. Tell me you don't want that," Steve grinned.

"No. I don't." *Do I?*

"Liar. Have a fun evening. I'll check on you in a bit." Steve walked away and left Laura to stew.

"Hey, can I get a diet soda?" Vic asked as he leaned backward against the bar. Laura hadn't seen him come up, and she jumped about a foot. "Damn, woman, I just want a drink. I'm not gonna slap you or anything. Calm down," he snapped, not even cracking a smile.

"Don't you want your usual beer?" she asked, surprised that he'd asked for a soft drink.

"Nope. Against the rules."

"Whose rules?" Laura asked.

"Mine." She sat the drink in front of him and he picked up the glass. She couldn't help but notice how elegant his hands were, long, strong fingers with just the lightest dusting of dark hair across them. Looking at them made her feel odd. "Can't drink alcohol and keep my wits about me with a sub."

"You're serious about this, aren't you?" Laura asked, her mouth hanging open.

The new Vic Cabrizzi looked into her eyes and asked, "And what would make you think I'm not?" The low growl in his voice made her insides quiver, and she had to look away. "That's exactly what I thought." He finished the drink and smacked the glass onto the bar, then walked away. *What the hell?*, Laura thought. She looked down and saw her hands – they were visibly shaking.

Several of the unattached women in the club spent most of the evening talking to Vic, but most of them wanted to be collared by a Dom – right that minute. And Vic was not interested in that at all. They could flirt all they wanted, but it got them nowhere. He made it clear: He was a service Dom, and he'd be glad to meet their needs, but that was it.

"Oh my god! He's so gorgeous!" one woman was gushing as she and another woman walked up to the bar. "Can I have a Bud Light?" she asked Laura, who pulled it and sat it down in front of her.

"I'd take him on in a New York minute," her friend said. "I needed a sign that said 'slippery when wet' just standing there talking to him!" Laura wanted to throw up.

"I want to climb up there and let him spank me good, but he's so damn big, he's kinda scary," the first one said. *Ha! Wish he could hear that!*, Laura thought.

But that left her wondering why she wanted him to fail. He'd obviously worked hard to train with Alex. She should be happy for him, that he was more confident and looked better, happier, than she'd ever seen him. Why did seeing him looking and feeling good make her feel so bad? *Maybe I'm the bitch that José said I am.*

Laura felt her phone vibrate in her pocket and she pulled it out to see an unfamiliar number on the screen. She'd advertised to try to find a roommate, and she hoped that someone was responding. When she answered the call, a male voice said something, but the club was too loud. "Hang on just a minute, please. I can't hear you." She looked around – no Steve. "Hey, Vic!" she yelled. Vic broke away from a beautiful, bare-breasted brunette and came over to the bar. "Hey, I've got a phone call. Can you watch the bar for just a minute?"

"Yeah, but just a minute. Get your ass right on back here," he said. He'd never talked to her like that before, and she was taken aback, but she didn't have time to worry about that.

Jetting out the side door behind the bar, she put the phone back up to her ear. "Yeah, sorry about that. Can I help you? Are you calling about the ad for a roommate."

"No." Something about the voice made her feel odd. "Laura? Laura Billings?" Her hands went cold and a buzzing started in her ears. "Billings?"

"Who the hell is this?" she growled into the phone.

"Laura, I'm so sorry to call you and drag all of this up. This is Brewster. Please don't hang up on me."

"DON'T CALL ME AGAIN!" Laura screamed into the phone, then hit END and dropped the phone on the ground. It promptly rang again; same number.

She stared at the phone. Everything was coming at her in a rush, and the earth seemed to tilt. She hit ACCEPT and asked through gritted teeth, "What the hell do you want?"

"Laura, please, don't hang up. I need to talk to you. I want to make this right; we all do. Well, almost all of us. I hear a lot of noise in the background. Can I call you later? Or tomorrow? It's important."

"I can't believe you'd have the nerve to call me. How did you find me?" she was whispering, feeling so weak that she could barely speak.

"Billings, I know it's hard to believe, but I want to make this right. It's eaten at me for years, ruined my life and I'm betting yours too, and it's time to man up. Please. Let me do this, me and the others. Please?"

Laura's head was spinning and she felt like she was going to throw up. It was a little late for an apology, but it was more than she'd gotten over the last sixteen years, sixteen years of sheer hell. "Call me tomorrow. Ten o'clock tomorrow morning. That's Eastern Time."

"Okay. Ten o'clock tomorrow morning. Will do." The phone went dead. Laura stood staring at the phone, her hands shaking so hard that she could barely hold it. After a minute or two, she walked back through the side door and up to the bar.

"Where the hell were you?" Vic barked. Then he got a good look at her face. "God, Laura, what's wrong?" She stared at the bar, and Vic grabbed her arms and spun her to look at him. "Talk to me. What is it?"

Laura shook his hands off. "Don't touch me. Leave me alone. Nothing's wrong." She grabbed the towel and started wiping.

She heard Vic say, "That's a lie. I don't believe it for a minute. And when you decide you need someone to talk to about whatever just happened, find me. I can't speak for anyone else, but you can *always* trust me. I'd never hurt you, not in a million years." Laura turned to apologize to him for the way she'd talked to him, but he was gone.

Vic walked into the men's locker room and leaned against the wall. He knew damn well something had happened, but the ice princess wasn't going to tell him what or take any help from anyone. And he was done with trying to get someone who didn't want to be around him to open up to him. That was a dead-end street, and he'd walked down too many of them already.

From Renovating a Heart,
Book 3 in the
Love Under Construction Series

An hour and fifteen minutes into his Wednesday work day, his phone buzzed. "Steve, your nine thirty appointment is here."

"Yeah, okay, it's . . ."

"Miss Markham?"

Steve wracked his brain – he didn't know a woman named Markham. "Send her on in." He put his jacket and his professional face on, then took his seat behind the big mahogany desk.

The door opened and Angela, Steve's assistant, ushered the woman in. Steve's eyes went wide and a huge smile spread across his face. "Kelly!"

"Hi Steve! Wow, nice office!"

"Thanks! I didn't recognize your last name. Glad to see you! Want something to drink?" She shook her head. "So what can I do for you?" he asked, motioning for her to sit in one of the chairs in front of his desk.

Pinkness spread across her cheeks and her hands shook as she pulled a document out of her purse. "I talked to Nikki. She said you were the person I needed to talk to; she said you'd understand." Steve unfolded the document she passed to him.

It was a submissive's contract. He blinked a couple of times to be certain he was seeing it correctly. Sure enough, the submissive's name was plain on the top of the document: Kelly Markham. Now he understood why Nikki had sent her to him. "This was very well done. Did he break the contract with you?"

"Sort of." Kelly's gaze fell to her hands in her lap. "He passed."

"Oh my god! I'm so sorry! How long ago was this?"

"Nine years." She sniffed. "I still miss him every day."

Steve came around from his desk chair to the armchair next to Kelly. "So how can I help?"

"He made this out thinking it would protect me. Then when he died and we weren't married, his kids took everything, even some of the gifts he'd given me over the years. I'm about the same age as they are, so they saw me as a gold-digger who just wanted him for his money. They even called me a pervert because they didn't understand our lifestyle. I would've married him if he'd ever asked, but he never did. But he loved me, he really did, and I loved him. Even though I could've used the money, I just gave up – it wasn't about money to start with.

And I've done okay until Friday when I lost my job. We think they want to close the branch of the insurance company where I worked, and they just laid me off. I've got three months' severance and I'll draw unemployment, but it's not much. I know Dom/sub contracts aren't legally binding, but I was wondering if . . ."

"No, they're not. But this one clearly shows intent. He genuinely thought he'd protected you by making this contract. I wish it had worked." Steve thought for a minute. "You know, I don't want to get your hopes up, but let me see if I can find something, a case precedent or a loophole, anything, that could help. Can I make a copy of this?"

"Sure! Please! How much will you charge me? Because I don't have any . . ."

"You're Nikki's friend, and you took Laura in when she needed a place to hide. Just consider this my way of repaying you."

"Oh, no, I couldn't . . ."

"Oh yes, you can and you will." Steve took the contract out to Angela and asked her to make him a copy. When he came back, he asked Kelly, "Did Nikki by any chance tell you . . ."

"That you're in the lifestyle? Yeah. That's why she told me to come and talk to you."

"Did she tell you that I have a fetish club in Lexington?" *Boy, I'd love to see her in nothing but a smile!*, he thought.

"No! She didn't! I'd love to visit sometime." Kelly's eyes were sparkling now.

"I'd love for you to visit. Just give me a call and let me know you're coming so I can be looking for you. I'd love to show you around."

"I'll do that. And thanks, Steve. I really appreciate this."

"No problem." As she left, he handed her a card for the club with his signature on the back. He was glad she'd come in, and he hoped she'd come by and like the club enough to stick around, because he was itching to see those tits bare. He knew they were fake, but they were real enough for him.

I hope you enjoyed these excerpts from the **Love Under Construction Series.** *Check your favorite online retailer for the format that works best with your electronic device.*

Connect with Deanndra on Substance B

Substance B is a new platform for independent authors to directly connect with their readers. Please visit Deanndra's Substance B page where you can:

- Sign up for Deanndra's newsletter
- Send a message to Deanndra
- See all platforms where Deanndra's books are sold
- Request autographed eBooks from Deanndra

Visit Substance B today to learn more about your favorite independent authors.

Made in the USA
Charleston, SC
14 April 2015